Bright Summaries.com

The Lesson

BY EUGÈNE IONESCO

Written by Baptiste Frankinet
Translated by Oliver Brown

The Lesson

by Eugène Ionesco

EUGENE IONESCO

FRENCH PLAYWRIGHT AND ESSAYIST

- **Born in 1909 in Slatina (Romania)**

- **Died in 1994 in Paris**

- **Some of his works:**

    - *The Bald Cantatrice* (1950), play

    - *Rhinoceros* (1959), play

    - *Le roi se meurt* (1962), play

Born of a Romanian father and a French mother, Eugène Ionesco arrived in France a year after his birth and was naturalised in France in 1951. His theatrical work (*La Cantatrice chauve*; *La Leçon,* 1951; *Les Chaises,* 1952, etc.) has left its mark on literature. Today, he is one of the most widely performed French playwrights in the world. Anxious to be understood, he has left many commentaries on his work (*Notes et contre-notes,* 1962; *Journal en miettes,* 1967, etc.). He was elected to the Académie française in 1970.

Ionesco is the leader of the theatre of the absurd, a new theatrical genre which, in the aftermath of the Second World War (1939-1945), overturned the rules of classical theatre.

THE LESSON

THE ABSURD LESSON OF A TEACHER TO HIS PUPIL

- **Genre:** theatre (tragedy)

- **Reference edition:** *La Leçon*, Paris, Gallimard, « Folio théâtre » collection, 1994, 131 p.

- **1ʳᵉ edition:** 1951

- **Themes:** temptation, murder, desire, language, power, teaching

The Lesson is a one-act play written in 1950 and performed a few months later. In it, Ionesco portrays an old teacher who receives a young student in his home for private lessons. As the play progresses, the lesson becomes more complicated and communication between teacher and student breaks down. The story ends with the murder of the young woman by her teacher.

Today, *The Lesson is* one of Eugène Ionesco's most performed and most read plays. This tragedy has the particularity of allowing everyone to interpret it in their own way.

SUMMARY

The play is not divided into scenes or acts. It is played by three characters: the teacher, the student and the teacher's maid.

A VERY SPECIAL LESSON

A young student planning to prepare for the "total doctorate competition" to satisfy her parents goes to a teacher for private lessons.

At first, they discuss banalities, an opportunity for the professor to test the girl's basic knowledge. When the girl tells the professor that she is 'at his disposal' (p. 33), she arouses desire in him, and it becomes clear that the relationship between the two characters is ambiguous. The lecherous nature of the teacher is emphasised in the didascalia (for example, his looks are often described as 'libidinous') and also appears in curious lines, such as when he explains mathematical operations by illustrating them with far-fetched examples that refer to the student's body: 'If you had had two noses, and I had torn one off… How many would you have left now?' (p. 45)

He then proceeds with a lesson in arithmetic. The lesson starts with a question-and-answer session. But the young student, who seemed brilliant at first, gradually reveals major gaps in her knowledge. Thus, when they discuss addition at the simplest level (1 + 1, 2 + 1, etc.), the teacher seems to marvel – excessively – at the fact that she has mastered this elementary level of knowledge. But when he considers subtraction, he realises that she is not able to think about simple data (she cannot solve 4 – 3 or know if 3 is greater than 4). Paradoxically, she is able to perform extremely complex calculations (p. 52), having memorised all the possible multiplications.

A PREMONITORY PAIN

The teacher is slightly exasperated by a success that is clearly not accompanied by the reflection traditionally required for this kind of exercise. After the arithmetic lesson, the philology lecture begins the deterioration of the relationship between teacher and student. Carried away by his impetus and irritated by the young woman's interruptions, the teacher becomes threatening.

The student only intervenes to complain endlessly about a toothache. The teacher calls the maid, who immediately sees in the student's pain a symptom of the fatal outcome of the lesson. She knows that this is not the first student who has turned up for a private lesson. In fact, this is already the fortieth time of the day that her boss has acted in this way, and it happens every day. She tries to intervene but is sent back to the kitchen.

TOWARDS A TRAGIC END

The teacher, out of his mind, insults and threatens, and starts a hypnosis session which evolves according to the demands of the word and the omnipotence of his own desire. While the teacher turns around her, the pupil is forced to repeat the same word over and over again, "knife", a fatal announcement of the fate that awaits her.

The young woman complains of pain in her throat, shoulders, breasts, hips, thighs and stomach. Finally, the man brandishes a knife; he rapes and kills her. As soon as the crime is committed, the teacher panics and calls his maid for help.

Distraught, he refuses to admit his wrongdoing. However, he is called to order by the maid who, like a mother, lectures him, tired of his behaviour. The teacher regrets and seems to deplore his actions, but a new student rings the doorbell, perpetuating an endless cycle...

CHARACTER STUDY

With the exception of the maid, named Marie, the other two characters are never named other than by their social function, i.e. "the teacher" and "the student".

At first glance, these characters, who have no identity and are reduced to their status alone, may seem flat and thin. However, the stage directions provide the reader with detailed information about their development over the course of the play, as well as the relationships they have with each other.

THE STUDENT

The 18-year-old girl is fresh and cheerful. Dressed in a "grey apron, small white collar", she has a "towel under her arm" as an accessory (p. 23). Her appearance thus described suggests that she comes from a good, probably bourgeois family, which is corroborated by her social background ("my parents are quite wealthy", p. 31; "young girl of the world", p. 26). Superficial, she seems to have no clear personal aspirations, her aim being above all to satisfy her parents by following the path they have set for her.

Her character evolves throughout the play; voluble, and self-confident. She gradually becomes destabilised and then overwhelmed by the teacher's attitude and questions, which she is unable to answer. She then gradually withdraws into herself. She feels overwhelmed. However, she tries to make herself heard by repeating the same words over and over again ("I have a toothache"), almost obsessively.

Her role in the play is all the more significant as it gives a particular dimension to her relationships: from the smooth and polite student of the beginning, she quickly finds herself overwhelmed by the situation, a victim of the professor's ascendancy, unassertive and unresponsive behaviour; a submission which is moreover reminiscent of her relationship with her parents, who in a way impose on her to take this exam ('My parents also want me to deepen my knowledge. They want me to specialise", p. 30; "My parents [...] would like me to get my full doctorate", p. 31). Finally, she appears as an interchangeable character; without a first or last name, inconsistent; she has no striking personality and blends in with the forty or so students who have preceded her and those who will succeed her with the professor.

THE TEACHER

"He is the stereotypical teacher, both in appearance and in his initially deferential attitude. His psychological portrait does not remain stable, however, but evolves considerably; from being ill at ease, shy, bordering on the ridiculous (his voice is "rather fluent", p. 24; the suspension points show his numerous hesitations when he searches for his words; a didascalia indicates that he stammers slightly), he then becomes domineering, and then perverse to the point of murder, before finding himself distraught like a little boy.

Socially, he embodies both authority and knowledge. The questions he asks the girl are, however, of a more than elementary level, and his pedagogy singular; he compliments his pupil excessively, before abusing his power, using, on the one hand, his status as a teacher to intimidate his pupil, and on the other hand, his status as a boss in order to dismiss his maid. This double dialectic of teacher/pupil and boss/housekeeper underlines his relational difficulties and his dangerously unstable attitude. Indeed, he first addresses the pupil in a very courteous manner ('I am only your servant', p. 33), addressing her in a polite manner, before going on to insult her, and finally threatening her ('No insolence, mignonne, or beware of you', p. 76), all of which will lead him to commit a murder.

The main character in *The Lesson*, clearly suffering from a split personality, embodies both absurdity and madness.

THE RIGHT

Marie, the teacher's maid, is a "strong" woman, "45 to 50 years old", "red-faced", who wears a "peasant headdress" (p. 23). She thus appears as a simple, uneventful maid in the service of her boss, and greets the pupil appropriately before the teacher arrives.

However, her psychological profile is no less complex. She shows a certain duplicity, especially in her relationship with the teacher. From a relational point of view, she certainly obeys her boss's orders but does not hesitate to leave her subordinate role to address him frankly, even to rush him. She intervenes on her own in two occasions to warn him. When she lingers in the room where the lesson is taking place, she warns him ('Be careful, I recommend calm', p. 34); 'Arithmetic […] it gets on your nerves', p. 35), and then disrupts the lesson again when the teacher turns to philology to tell him that 'philology leads to the worst' (p. 55), before warning him one last time by mentioning 'the final symptom! The big symptom!" (p. 79). Moreover, in the end, she does not hesitate to reprimand her boss by being 'sarcastic' and 'very harsh' (p. 85), before taking pity on him and reassuring him.

The evolution of this character is cyclical in that, in the end, she reverts to being the affable and respectful maid who welcomes a new pupil in the same way she welcomed the previous one while being aware of the risks involved.

KEYS TO READING

NARRATIVE OUTLINE

Initial situation: this is the beginning of the story, the moment when the setting is set and the characters are introduced; the situation is balanced, i.e. it has no reason to change.

- Arrival of the student welcomed by the maid before the beginning of the private lesson.

Disruptive element: this is an event that disrupts the initial situation and triggers the story itself.

- The ambiguity of the student's words ("I am at your disposal", p. 33), which gives rise to libidinous impulses in the teacher.

Peripherals: these are the events caused by the disturbing element and which lead to the action(s) taken by the hero to solve the problem.

- The teacher's agitation and excitement, initially uncomfortable, increase as he tackles different subjects; the maid's interventions, warning her boss with more or less implicit remarks; the teaching of arithmetic and then philology, accompanied by a tenfold increase in the teacher's verbal violence; the student's incessant complaints about having a toothache; the teacher's growing tension around the word "knife", which he makes his hypnotised student repeat.

Denouement: brings the events to an end and leads to the final situation.

- Rape and murder of the girl by her teacher at the end of a confusing lecture.

Final situation: this is the end of the story. The situation is again stable, like the initial situation, but it has undergone transformations.

- The teacher panics and is soon joined by his maid who mentions the burial of forty other students, before the arrival of a new student.

A TRAGEDY?

From the outset, Ionesco presents his play as a comic drama. It is true that he respects certain characteristics of classical tragedy: there is only one main action (a lesson given by a teacher to his pupil) that takes place in one place (the teacher's house) and in a fairly short period of time. The plot follows a normal dramatic progression:

- an exhibition, during which the framework of the story is set;

- a knot that is gradually created in the relationship between the teacher and the student;

- an ending that is marked by the death of the student.

Moreover, as in classical tragedy, the reader/spectator can easily perceive the fate of the student through the textual clues that appear in the dialogue. Moreover, the student more than frequently uses the register of lamentation ("Oh, no! Oh, dear! I've had enough! And then my teeth hurt, my feet hurt, my head hurts", p. 80) and, as soon as she loses control over her interlocutor, she uses an anguished register, full of hesitations ("My grandmother's roses are also… yellow, in French, ça dit jaune? "(p. 67); « Les… comment dit "roses" en roumain? » (p. 70); "Excuse me, sir, but… […] I don't know the difference" (*id.*).

However, several elements prevent us from affirming that this is a real tragedy. There are many comical elements that mitigate the tragic value of the play:

- ridicule is omnipresent in the lessons of arithmetic and philology;

- The student is far removed from the classical tragic hero; she is unaware of the fate that awaits her and, far from acting courageously in the face of that fate, she seems to resign herself and submit totally to the goodwill of her teacher;

- the murder shown on stage does not respect the rule of propriety which consists in not showing anything shocking to the public;

- The tragic aspect is totally relativised by the last words of the play. As soon as the maid tells us that this is the fortieth murder committed and that it happens every day, the drama of the scene depicted disappears completely and is replaced by absurdity. The denouement-recommencement removes the tragedy from the murder scene and turns it into a non-event, a meaningless fact.

GRATING COMEDY

The subtitle of the play, 'Comic Drama', also refers to the comic register. This is confirmed throughout the play. Numerous devices are used to give this tragedy comic, even burlesque connotations. Most of them are related to the teacher.

To the ridiculous character of the professor with the "thin voice" (p. 24) is added his initial attitude: he constantly apologises: "I don't know how to apologise for keeping you waiting… I was just finishing… wasn't I, from… I apologise… You'll excuse me" (p. 27). His unease is pervasive. Suspension points abound, perhaps portraying a slight stammer. He is hesitant, searching for words.

There was also a discrepancy between the "total doctorate competition" prepared by the student and the level of the very basic questions asked by the teacher. For example, he asks her about seasons and then makes her add up the numbers. As for subtractions, the girl is not able to solve them. The teacher's comments are often off the mark, even meaningless (e.g. when he says that he would like to live in Bordeaux, even though he does not know the city, p. 27-28). His logic and pedagogy are whimsical.

At the beginning of the play, the teacher constantly uses exaggeration, a fundamental element of the comic register. He apologises repeatedly and without reason: 'I don't know how to apologise [...]. I apologise… You will excuse me…" (p. 27); "My apologies." (*id.*); "Courage… miss… I apologise… patience" (p. 28); "I apologise, miss, I was going to tell you" (p. 29); "I apologise for having to contradict you" (p. 39). He marvels at his pupil's very rudimentary and incomplete knowledge; he pays her exaggerated, inappropriate compliments: "But yes, Miss, bravo, but that's very good, it's perfect. My congratulations', p. 28); 'Magnifique! You are magnificent! You are exquisite. I congratulate you warmly, Miss. [...] As for the bill, you are masterful" (p. 39). He also uses hyperbole very often, for example when he is concerned to know whether his pupil is not "exhausted" after having made her add up ("Tell me, only, if you are not exhausted, how much is four minus three?", *ibid.*).

His words are often inappropriate, even indecent, especially after the murder of the girl: "Not too expensive, all the same, the crowns. She hasn't paid her lesson. (p. 88) Finally, elements are mentioned that do not exist, such as the "total doctorate competition" or the "supra-total diploma".

Through this character, the comedy of the play becomes absurd.

THE DESTRUCTION OF LANGUAGE

As in *The Bald Cantatrice*, Ionesco seeks to destroy the communicative function of language. He uses various means to achieve this:

- Firstly, it features two characters who discuss without really listening to each other: the teacher, for example, talks about consonants 'changing their nature in slurs', while the student repeats that she has a toothache, and continues without taking this into account ('Let's go on', p. 61). The main function of language is thus reduced to nothing and only reappears after the murder;

- secondly, Ionesco overdevelops conventional language that is meaningless outside the context in which it operates. The polite formulas, for example, are multiplied. They are used to measure who has the upper hand. At the beginning of the play, the teacher uses as many 'Misses' as possible, but at the end of the play, the pupil begs with countless 'Sirs'. Moreover, the teacher uses many insults, which are not very appropriate to the context in which the scene takes place;

- Finally, the frequent repetitions make certain scenes lose all meaning and allow the introduction of the absurdity of the language.

This absurdity of language is very present in the translation lesson. The teacher teaches his pupil the word 'knife' in all languages, before making her repeat it in one language, French. Moreover, he claims to be teaching her 'neo-Spanish', an idiom that does not exist. This scene is therefore representative of the meaninglessness of the dialogue between the student and the teacher. Similarly, the incessant repetition of the word "knife" empties it of its meaning and turns it into an onomatopoeia. The sounds [k] and [t] evoke, as Ionesco suggests in his didascalia, the mechanical ticking of a clock.

LANGUAGE AS A SYMBOL OF POWER

In *The Lesson*, the two characters seem to belong to two different worlds. One, a dominant, violent man, insists on teaching an incomprehensible subject to the other, who is dominated, does not want to listen and remains totally focused on herself. The teacher, exasperated by the lack of control he has over his pupil, uses language as a means of possessing the other. His position as a teacher gives him authority over his interlocutor and, through the authority of language and his knowledge, he manages to dominate her completely and ends up killing his student.

The word, at first governed by polite formulas and kindly behaviour, gradually escapes all measure, until it makes the murderous object – the knife – real. Indeed, the knife does not exist materially; it is the representative force of the word that succeeds in murdering the girl.

Finally, it is indeed the dialogue that leads the professor to a kind of schizophrenia. Once the murder has been carried out, he acts as if he has woken up and an unconscious double has acted in his place. He reverts to the shy and impressionable character he was and refuses to believe that he was capable of such an act.

A SATIRE OF EDUCATION

The play also offers a caricature of education. Ionesco has fun showing that the language that serves as the main vehicle for teaching can be completely meaningless. For example, when the teacher proposes to analyse the proverbial expression 'falling on deaf ears', he says: 'Sounds, Mademoiselle, must be caught on the fly by the wings so that they do not fall on deaf ears. Therefore, when you decide to articulate, it is advisable, as far as possible, to raise your neck and chin very high, to stand on tiptoe, so you see…" (p. 59) Thus, the teacher, contrary to what his profession would require of him, sticks to a first-degree understanding of the expression he is trying to explain.

Moreover, he often adopts a magisterial tone to explain things that he tries to present as logical and which, however, are totally implausible. He mentions, for example, a certain comrade who suffered from a pronunciation defect: 'He couldn't pronounce the letter f. Instead of f, he said f. So instead of font, he said f. Instead of f, he would say f. Thus, instead of fountain, I will not drink your water, he would say: fountain, I will not drink your water. (p. 63) On reading, there is obviously no difference between these two sentences. Similarly, when they consider the different translations of the word 'knife': 'It will be enough if you pronounce the word knife in all languages' (p. 79), and later, 'Ah, if you insist, neck, knife. It's neo-Spanish...', 'If you like, yes, neo-Spanish, [...] And then, what is this useless question?' (p. 81).

AN INEXORABLE OUTCOME

Clues scattered throughout the play to announce the macabre denouement to come. The rhythm becomes progressively frantic, the lines are exchanged without answering each other in a kind of stichomythia, a sequence from which the suspension points that we saw at the beginning of the play have completely disappeared.

The maid's warnings, at first mysterious and implicit ("Be careful, I recommend calm", p. 34; "You won't say I didn't warn you", p. 35), become clearer as the teacher gains the upper hand over the pupil, dominates her and drags her into the wake of her madness.

The teacher's own seemingly innocuous warnings take on a whole new meaning in light of her crime: "You will learn that anything can be expected. (p. 29) Later, he threatens her: 'Don't make me angry! I won't answer for myself anymore." (p. 72); then, speaking of her teeth: "I'll pull them out for you!" (p. 74). The threat then becomes clearer: "Silence! Or I'll smash your skull" (*id.*); "I'm going to rip your ears off, so they won't hurt anymore, my sweet!" (p. 81)

The lecherous nature of the professor is mentioned in the first few lines ('the lecherous gleam in his eyes will eventually become a consuming, unbroken flame', p. 26).

References to the girl's body parts multiply: two sense organs, the nose and then the ear, are first evoked, serving to illustrate the lesson ('If you had had two noses, and I would have torn one of them off you…', p. 45; then, alluding to her ears: 'You have two, I take one, I eat one of them', id.).

Some lines make clearer references to death, for example when the teacher tells the student: "Remember this until the time of your death…" (p. 59), to which she innocently replies: "Oh yes, sir, until the time of my death", thereby endorsing his words without really being aware of it. Finally, the appearance of the (invisible) knife that he takes from a drawer and brandishes foreshadows the worst ("He brandished the knife in front of the student's eyes", p. 80; "the knife kills…", p. 83). Then, the violence of the uncontrollable word becomes physical violence: the power of the words has reached the flesh, and the scene will be replayed – until exhaustion?

A WORK REPRESENTATIVE OF THE THEATRE OF THE ABSURD

Offbeat and burlesque, *The Lesson* features human types, or rather characters who appear dehumanised, lacking their own identity, caricatured to excess, and plays on the themes of death and absurdity. These are themes that are often found in the theatre of the absurd.

According to the critic Martin Esslin, 'the theatre of the absurd shows [the human condition] simply in existence, i.e. concrete images illustrate the absurdity of existence on stage' (*Encyclopaedia of Literature*, Paris, Le Livre de Poche, 2003, pp. 4-5). It can be added here that the absurdity of the play lies in the incommunicability, or rather the difficulty of communicating between the characters, insofar as we are often faced with a dialogue of the deaf. This is significant in *The Lesson* insofar as the student complains about his physical pain, with words that fall into a void, like a litany of nothingness.

Furthermore, Ionesco, who 'plays on all the registers of the illogicality of language', 'transforms man into a pontificating puppet' (*id.*), which is the case of the teacher in *The Lesson*.

Finally, according to Pascal Riendeau, "the plays [of the theatre of the absurd] are united by their unusual character and mix tragic elements and comic situations in an unusual way," traits that are found in Ionesco's play: even if the end is fateful, the hilarious words and incongruous situations bring *The Lesson* to a level where the absurd only aims to confine the characters to their dehumanised condition.

THE RECEPTION OF THE WORK

Considered or perceived as too avant-garde, Ionesco's *The Lesson* was not an immediate success, either from the point of view of the public or of the critics. Ionesco was an unknown author at the time, as were the actors and director.

Although the play received a lukewarm reception at its first two performances at the Théâtre de Poche on 20 February 1951, and then at the Théâtre Lancry in the spring of 1952, it had its first success at the Théâtre de la Huchette on 7 October 1952, when director Jacques Noël had the idea of combining *La Leçon* with Ionesco's first play, *La Cantatrice chauve*.

It was in 1957 that the play, which is always performed after *The Bald Cantress*, was a success. Audiences and critics alike were unanimous, and since then, *The Lesson* has been performed continuously and translated into all languages. It continues to be performed all over the world.

For the playwright, the comic and tragic registers are inseparable, even interchangeable, which explains the complexity and ambiguity of his plays on the one hand, and the unexpected reaction of the audience on the other.

AVENUES FOR REFLECTION

A FEW QUESTIONS FOR FURTHER REFLECTION...

- Identify the characteristics of the absurd in this play. Justify this.

- Describe the three characters. Imagine what they symbolise given the historical and political context of the time, as the play was written in 1950.

- What weapon does the teacher use to murder his student? Why do you think Ionesco states in a didascalia that this weapon may be imaginary?

- Note the presence of different objects in *The Lesson*. What form do they take and what role do they play in this play? Can you draw a parallel with the play *Les Chaises*?

- Explain the role of language in this play and compare it to the role it plays in other plays by Ionesco.

- Look for clues throughout the play that announce the ending.

- Identify the comic elements in the play. What is their purpose?

- Can we say that *The Lesson* is a tragedy?

- It has been argued that *The Lesson* is a play of meta-morphosis. What is your opinion? Justify your answer with examples.

- *The Lesson* is a play of the absurd. Compare it to other plays of the same movement such as *The Bald Cantatrice* or *Waiting for Godot* (1952) by Samuel Beckett (Irish writer, 1906-1989). Point out the differences and similarities between these plays.

TO GO FURTHER

REFERENCE EDITION

Ionesco E., *La Leçon*, Paris, Gallimard, « Folio théâtre » collection, 1994.

BENCHMARK STUDIES

Esslin M., *Le théâtre de l'absurde*, Paris, Éditions Buchet Chastel, 1992.

Encyclopedia of Literature, Le Livre de Poche, 2003.

Ionesco E., *Notes et contre-notes*, Paris, Gallimard, « Folio essais » collection, 1966.

"The story", in *Théâtre de la Huchette*, accessed on 4 November 2011. http://www.theatre-huchette.com/un-peu-dhistoire/spectacle-ionesco/lhistoire/

Riendeau P., « Absurde (théâtre de l') », in *Le Dictionnaire du littéraire*, Paris, PUF, 2002.

Your opinion is important to us!
Leave a comment on the website of your online bookshop
and share your favourites on social networks!

www.brightsummaries.com

Ebook EAN: 9782808686488
Paperback EAN: 9782808697880
Legal Deposit: D/2023/12603/1068

Cover: © Primento
Digital conception by Primento, the digital partner of publishers.